MAY 03 2021

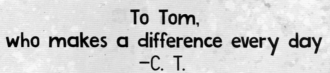

To Tom,
who makes a difference every day
—C. T.

To my beautiful mother, Joann Darlene.
She taught me to believe in cyclical compassion,
and she always shares her food with everyone (even if it's the best bite)
—K. J.

With special thanks to Josh Rieders

A NOTE ABOUT SEA STARS:
Sea stars are beautiful and delicate creatures that live and breathe underwater.
If you discover a sea star on the beach, it should be handled with care
with gloves or clean hands (free of lotions and sunscreens).
Please do not take them out of the water for any reason—they don't like it!

The illustrations in this book were made digitally with multimedia.

Cataloging-in-Publication Data has been applied for and may be obtained from the Library of Congress.

ISBN 978-1-4197-4226-2

Text copyright © 2021 Christian Trimmer
Illustrations copyright © 2021 Kaylani Juanita
Book design by Pamela Notarantonio and Hana Anouk Nakamura

Printed and bound in China
10 9 8 7 6 5 4 3 2

Abrams Books for Young Readers are available at special discounts when purchased in quantity
for premiums and promotions as well as fundraising or educational use. Special editions can also be created
to specification. For details, contact specialsales@abramsbooks.com or the address below.

ABRAMS The Art of Books
195 Broadway, New York, NY 10007
abramsbooks.com

The Little Things

A STORY ABOUT ACTS OF KINDNESS

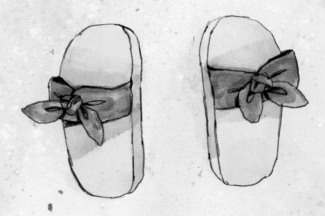

Words by CHRISTIAN TRIMMER

Art by KAYLANI JUANITA

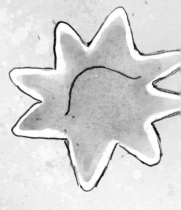

ABRAMS BOOKS FOR YOUNG READERS
NEW YORK

A little girl, who much preferred the look of three pigtails to two and who loved the way wet sand squished between her toes, walked down the dock the day after a mighty storm.

There, on the beach, were thousands of sea stars washed ashore by the violent waves.

She raced to one and tossed it back into the ocean.

She quickly picked up another

and another

and another,

ushering each back into
the safety of the water.

Just then, an old man, who had the habit of misplacing his glasses and who also loved the way wet sand squished between his toes, came by. "What are you doing, little girl?" he asked.

"WHAT DO YOU MEAN, WHAT AM I DOING?"
shouted the girl who liked three pigtails
and sand between her toes. She
also had a strong sense of self.
"I'm saving these sea stars!"

"I, uh, I was..." The old man was taken aback. "It's just, there are so many sea stars. What's the point? You won't be able to save them all."

"Of course I can't save them all," replied the little girl.

She carefully tossed another sea star into the ocean. "But I saved that one, didn't I?"

The old man had to admit the little girl had a point. He picked up a sea star and placed it back in the water.

Later that day, the old man headed to the animal shelter with his grandson, who liked butter on his noodles and brightly colored shoelaces.

"What are we doing here, Grandpa?" asked the little boy.

"I'm going to rescue a dog!" the old man replied.

The boy looked around. There were many animals who needed rescuing after the storm. "Taking home one dog isn't going to make much of a difference," he said.

"That may be so," his grandpa replied, "but it sure will make a difference to this little guy, don't you think?"

The little boy had to admit his grandpa had a point.

The next day, after a lunch of buttered noodles, the boy
headed to his neighbor's house. There lived an elderly lady, who
had once been a professional dancer and who loved butterflies.

"I'm here to clean up your garden," the little boy said to the elderly lady.

The storm had torn up her flowerbeds and tossed garbage all over her yard.
"That would be lovely," replied the elderly lady, doing a graceful plié.

As the little boy worked, a teenager, who listened to classical music very loudly on her headphones and who just couldn't be bothered, happened by.

"Hey, kid," she said, taking off her headphones. "What are you doing?"

"I'm cleaning up this lady's yard," he replied.

"Look around, kid. The storm messed up this whole block. What's the point of cleaning one yard?" asked the teenager, even though the kid *was* doing a good job.

Not that she'd ever say that to him.

The elderly lady chimed in. "This little boy has done more than just clean my yard, young lady," she said. "He has lifted my spirits. You could learn a thing or two from him."

The elderly lady had a point, though the teenager would *never* admit that out loud. Still, she gave the woman a nod and the little boy a high five.

The next morning, the teenager packed an extra lunch . . .

and gave it to the homeless man outside the coffee shop,
even though she knew there were many in need of a meal.

Then a little girl with one missing front tooth
and another wiggly one . . .

. . . took all the money she had received from the Tooth Fairy and gave it to charity (and she wiggled the other tooth to help it along).

The little girl's mom, who made scrumptious cupcakes, gooey brownies, and mouth-watering cookies (along with some equally delicious gluten-free options),

quickly organized a fundraiser,

which inspired a young man, with a great sense of style and real acting chops, to volunteer at the school,

which moved a whole class of students to donate their time
to fix up a house that had been damaged by the storm,

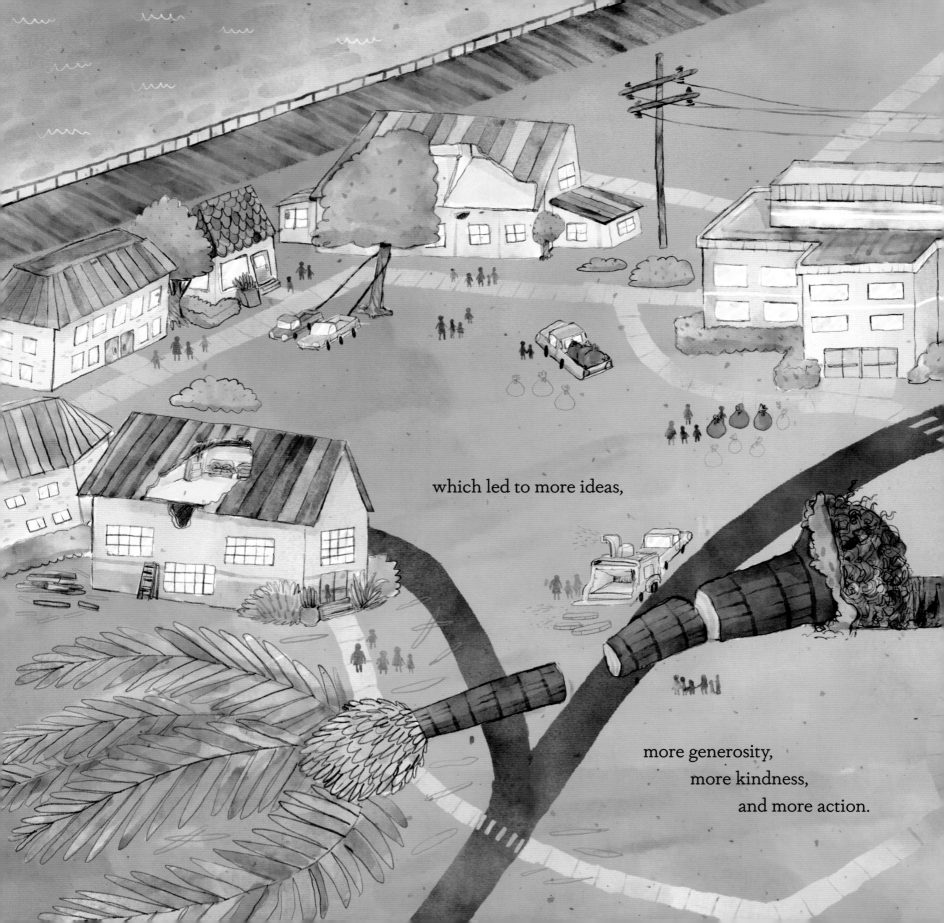

which led to more ideas,

more generosity,
more kindness,
and more action.

Not too long after that, another storm moved through the town.

The next morning, the little girl with three pigtails raced to the end of the dock, only to find . . .

The little girl walked up to the old man and gently tapped him on the shoulder. "Now do you get it?" she asked.

The old man did.